Calico's Curious Kittens

Phyllis Limbacher Tildes

SCHOLASTIC INC.

New York Toronto London Auckland Sydney
Mexico City New Delhi Hong Kong Buenos Aires

For Beverly Anderson Twigg,
my very first friend,
and in memory of her dog, Brandy

ISBN 0-439-66523-X

12 11 10 9 8 7 6 5 4 3 2 1   4 5 6 7 8 9/0

Printed in the U.S.A.   40

First Scholastic printing, March 2004

Illustrations in this book done in watercolor
on Arches Bright White 300 lb. hot press paper

Display type and text type set in Edwardian
and Sabon

Designed by Phyllis Limbacher Tildes

Pumpkin

Ginger

Frisky

Patch

Binky

Puff

Cally

Calico's kittens are curious.
They should be napping, but . . .

Ginger is in a bag.
Pumpkin is in a drawer.
Where is Frisky?

In trouble.

Uh, oh . . .

Here comes Mama Calico!
Ginger leaps out of the bag.
Pumpkin jumps out of the drawer.

Frisky needs a bath.

What does Frisky see?
Ginger and Pumpkin
jump up to look.

Up the curtains they go.

"Come up, Puff!"

Puff doesn't dare.

Calico meows, "Naughty kittens!"

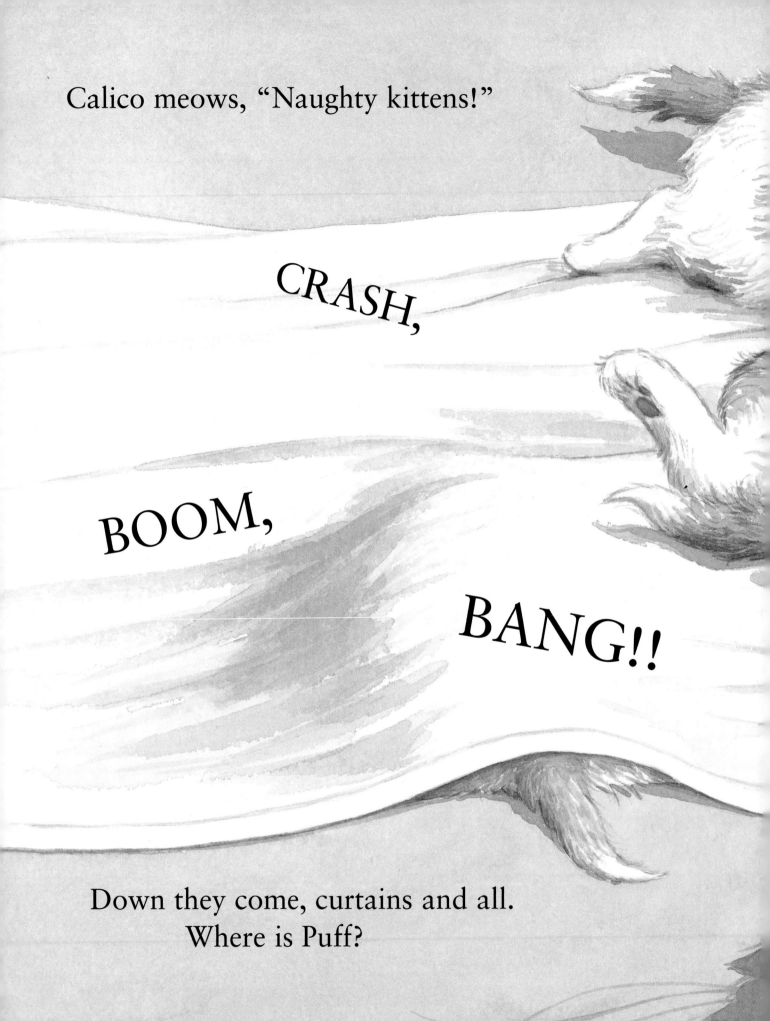

CRASH,

BOOM,

BANG!!

Down they come, curtains and all.
Where is Puff?

"Naptime!" says Calico.
"I'm not tired," says Frisky.

Frisky sneaks through the kitty door.
Binky, Patch, and Cally follow him.
Binky gets stuck, but Patch pushes
him through.

Frisky leads Binky, Patch, and Cally
across the little bridge
and across the lawn.

Cally pounces on Patch.

Binky jumps on Cally.

Frisky climbs on top.

Then one by one, they roll off.

Patch follows Cally around a tree.

Bees buzz around Binky.

What is this?

A dog!
Frisky scoots under the shed.
Patch hides under the bench.
Binky runs under the
wheelbarrow.

The dog wants to play.
He leaps over the bench.
He jumps over the
wheelbarrow.

Three curious kittens
creep too close.

The dog licks each soggy kitten.

But where is Cally?

"Meow!" Cally calls from above.
Hold on tight, Cally.

Far below, the dog barks for help.

Here comes Calico.

Binky hides behind Frisky.

Patch hides behind Binky.

Calico climbs the tree to rescue Cally.

The naughty kittens follow
Mama back inside the house.

They are finally ready for a nap.